The Book of
HOB
Stories

For Rachel and John Tomlinson
W. M.

For my parents
P. B.

First U.S. edition in this form 1997
Library of Congress Cataloging-in-Publication Data
Mayne, William, date.
The book of Hob stories / William Mayne ; illustrated by Patrick Benson.—1st U.S. ed.
Summary: Hob, the friendly spirit who lives under the stairs and protects the house,
must do battle with a variety of evil beings trying to take control of his family's home.
ISBN 0-7636-0390-2
[1. Fairies—Fiction.] I. Benson, Patrick, ill. II. Title.
PZ7.M4736Bo   1997
[Fic]—dc21   96-52907

2 4 6 8 10 9 7 5 3 1

Printed in Hong Kong

This book was typeset in Goudy.
The pictures were done in watercolor and ink.

Candlewick Press
2067 Massachusetts Avenue
Cambridge, Massachusetts 02140

The Book of
HOB
Stories

William Mayne
Illustrated by Patrick Benson

CANDLEWICK PRESS
CAMBRIDGE, MASSACHUSETTS

CONTENTS

Hob and Boggart

Who lit a twiggy fire in the ashes of the hearth
and filled the house with smoke in the middle
of the night?

Mr. asks the question, Mrs. wants to know.
Boy and Girl did not do it and cannot tell.

Budgie knows and shouts it out. Baby sees and yells the name, but no one understands.

"We'll go back to bed," says Mr. "I hope it's not your friend."

Boy and Girl know kindly Hob lives in his cutch, or cupboard, in the stairs. They know he did no such thing.

"No," says Hob. "But I'm about. Hob is where he thinks he is."

Mr. and Mrs. and Boy and Girl go back to bed.

"I saw it, I saw it," says Budgie.

Hob jumps up and makes a face at her. He thinks Budgie is a noise and not a thing. He is quiet himself and does not like a noise.

"Who is it?" he asks. But Budgie tucks her head under her wing and will not reply.

Hob goes to ask Baby.

"Wug, wug, wug," says Baby. Only Baby understands. Hob makes a face at it, and Baby laughs. Hob goes to find out for himself.

He listens. Something bumps about the house. Hob hears the milk go sour. Something rattles at a door. Hob hears the bread go moldy. Something shuffles across a floor. Hob hears the butter going wrong. Treading down the stairs he hears a scratching down below. There is something climbing into his cutch, his living place.

Hob is angry now. He goes right down. He thinks

he knows what this thing is. Budgie
has fainted quite away, her feathers
turning white.

"It made a face at me," she croaks.

"It's one of those," says Hob. "Hob thinks we'll have
a fight."

There, climbing into the cutch, is a fat and ugly

Boggart with really wicked eyes, bringing trouble and noise to Hob's own lucky house.

"Good night, Hob," says Boggart. "You'll have to move."

But Hob knows how to deal with Boggart. "We're all off," he says, cheerfully. "We're flitting, don't you know. We're doing it to trick you."

"Silly Hob to tell me, then," says Boggart, climbing out. "Where do we go?"

"Wait a bit," says Hob, and out he goes for a wheelbarrow and puts a box on it. "Room for you in here," says Hob, and Boggart clambers in, mean and greedy. Hob wheels him away.

"What a trick," says Boggart. "They don't want me and here I am."

"What a trick," says Hob. "Here we are," and tips the barrow in the river, box, Boggart, and all, and they float away. "Wet house," says Boggart, and Hob says, "Good-bye."

Hob goes home to see what Boy and Girl had left him. He hopes it is not clothes, or he will have to go. "If they cover Hob's back, he's off down the track," he says. But they left a twist of baccy. He smokes it by the chimney.

"Home, sweet home," he says, among kindly folk.

HOB AND NOBODY

"It is a lucky house," says Mr., coming down the
morning stairs.

"A happy house," says Mrs.

"We like it here," say Boy and Girl. "And we
know why." They think that friendly Hob lives
underneath the stairs in a little cutch, or cupboard.

"What nonsense, then," says Mr. "Now, where
are my vest and my hat? Who has seen them?"

Nobody has seen them.

"And where are my apron and the tea cozy?"
says Mrs. "Who has moved them?"

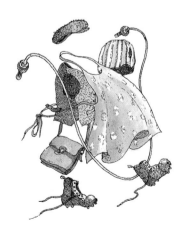

Nobody has moved them.

"And where," says Boy, "are
my soccer boots and my
satchel?"

Nobody has touched them.

"And where are my ribbons
and my skipping rope?"
says Girl.

Nobody knows.

Baby calls out for his bottle.

Nobody hears.

Hob in his cutch fast asleep wakes up and wonders.

"Hob has heard," he says. "Hob and Nobody. Nobody knows better, and Nobody knows worse."

Mr. finds his vest and his hat.

Mrs. finds her apron and the tea cozy.

Boy finds his soccer boots and his satchel.

Girl finds her ribbons and her skipping rope.

They have all been put tidy by the fireside.

"Mischief did that," says Mr., looking at Boy and Girl.

"Nobody knows," says Mrs.

"Nobody cares," says Budgie in her cage.

"Nobody won't give me my bottle," says Baby in his cradle, and Nobody understands him, or Budgie.

Hob looks from his spyhole in the side of the cutch. "I wish Hob was more real," he says. "I'd go down and talk to  them. But tonight I'll tell Nobody not to do it. This is meant to be a lucky house."

Mr. dresses in his vest and his hat; Mrs. puts on her apron and makes the tea. Boy goes to school with his boots, and Girl with her ribbons. Baby kicks in the cradle.

That night they are asleep when Hob comes out. He looks for Nobody. He knows what Nobody did. Nobody gave him clothes, vest, apron, boots, ribbons.

"Nobody wants Hob to go away," says Hob.
He knows what he knows. "Hob on the road begging
a lift, things to wear are a parting gift."

He finds Nobody in the dark, putting things in
the wrong places. "Hey, Nobody," says Hob.

"Mr. Nobody," says Nobody. "If you please."

"Mr. Nobody, come with me," says Hob. "I'll find

a happy nowhere place for you." And Hob puts him where Nobody goes, in the corners of the loft, down the sides of chairs, behind the water tank. Nobody doesn't mind spiders.

"There," says Hob. Budgie is so glad she claps hands and falls off her perch.

"Hob is the lucky one," says Hob, and drinks the milk Boy and Girl leave for him. "Hob is lucky. This is home."

HOB AND THE BLACK HOLE

Girl sits down to do her darning. "My heels and toes came through," she says. She sits on sleeping Hob in a chair by the fire. "Oh, Hob, I'm sorry," says Girl. "It is too dark to see you."

"Do your work and don't pretend," says Mrs.

"There's such a lot to mend just now."

"I sat on poor Hob," says Girl. Hob gets up and walks to his own cutch, or cubbyhole. "Look," says Girl.

"I can't see that," says Mrs. And then they mend and darn.

Hob gets into his cutch. He slept in the chair because the cutch is drafty.

There is a hole in the wall, not his eyehole spyhole, but a big and cold one. He shivers.

Mr. says, "There's a round hole in the window, very strange."

Boy says, "There's water in my shoe, a hole in the sole."

"There's something about," says Hob. "Hob knows the signs." He closes his eyes until night.

Then something crawls up to Budgie. Budgie worries. She can't see it. "It's trying to get into the cage," she squeals.

"It can have you," says Hob.

Budgie rings her bell and he has to go to help. There is something on the cage. Hob cannot see it, either. He can only see there's nothing there. There is an empty space. The empty space is sucking up Budgie's seeds.

"What are you doing here?" Hob asks. "Hob wants to know."

"Don't talk," says Budgie. "Peck it to death."

"I'm lost," says the thing. "I'm a baby black hole. I can't eat hard things like Mummy can, and I feel ill, and I want to go home."

"No wonder you feel ill," says Hob. "You have been eating toes of socks and soles of shoes."

"I was lying on the floor," says the baby black hole.

"On your way up here you ate the side of my cutch," says Hob. "But come with me. We'll find your mummy."

Very carefully he picks the baby black hole from the side of the cage. If a black hole nips you, that piece has gone forever. He takes it outside in the night, and the baby black hole looks at the big black sky.

"Mummy," it calls. "I see you, all that black."

But a star comes out, so Mummy is not there; and another comes, and she is not there either; and more and more. The baby black hole cries a little tear into itself. And all the sky comes bright. Except for one dark corner. And that corner comes nearer and closer

and picks up the baby black hole, and off they go
together, Mummy black hole and baby black hole.

Hob goes in and counts himself. He is all there.
Black holes never leave you a present. But Boy and
Girl have left him a piece of wood to mend his cutch.
"Can't eat it," says Hob. "But I'm not hungry,
somehow," and off he goes to bed with it.

HOB AND THE SAD

Who sent a card to Hob one winter, in snow,
when Christmas comes to people? Was it
friend Lob?

"Does Hob live here?" the postman asks.

"Yes," say Boy and Girl.

"What nonsense, then," says Mr.

Mrs. says the children have their fun, and Baby
says, "Happy Bubble," and Budgie sings a carol.

Boy puts the card for Hob in Hob's place, his
cutch, or den. He sleeps by day and keeps the
house by night.

"Well," says Hob when he wakes up, "Time
has remembered me," and reads his card to Budgie.
It is all Hobbish words. Budgie sings Budgie words
to Hob.

Hob goes to see what has gone on that day.
He finds parcels not for him. He finds trimmings
on a tree, paper chains across the
room, and holly by
the wall.

"Give us a kiss," says
Budgie, underneath
the mistletoe.

Hob makes a face at her. He is looking for
something that should be there. The people had been
nearly happy as they made Christmas ready, but not
quite so. Something had been sad.

Hob finds the Sad. It is hiding by the fireside,
a miserable lump, padding up and down on four
small legs.

"I feel so flat," it says. "So sad. It's my work, I know, but I don't like it."

"Tell Hob what it has to do," says Hob. "Hob has to know."

"Oh, oh, oh," says the Sad. "Look on the table."

"I see there flour and milk, egg and sugar, yeast and currants. That's work for Hob to do. By the fire they leave rewards. Hob don't care for salt and stitches, he's off in a moment if you give him britches. I see an egg on the table. It's not for him, but Hob loves an egg."

"It's all for me," says Sad. "I make bread hard and cake sink in the middle, and nothing will cure me."

"Tomorrow they have Christmas," says Hob. "Have you tried dancing, little Sad?"

"I tread on my own feet," says Sad.

"Have you sung a song?"

"Yes, but I bit my tongue."

Hob climbs to his cutch. He brings out a wooden flute and a wooden spoon. First he takes the wooden spoon. This is his work. He mixes egg and milk and sugar, flour, fat, and fruit.

"A waste of time," says Sad.

"Time sent me a card," says Hob. "Jump in, Sad, my stirring's nearly done."

Sad holds his breath and tumbles in.

"I'll spoil your work," he says.

Hob plays the flute. The dough moves and rises, lifts itself and swings about.

"Oh, I am charmed," says Sad, "I am cured," and the dough comes high in the bowl and smiles.

Hob pops it in the oven to be ready in the morning. "They'll want a turkey, too," he says to Budgie, who sulks at him.

Hob has his reward, a stocking with an apple.
He reads his card. It says, "Happy wishes Hob a
New Year."

HOB AND BLACK DOG

Girl keeps her room tidy, sweeps her floor, washes her face. She finds sixpence in her shoe.

"It's my reward for being clean," she says, "I got it from our Hob."

"Someone dropped it, I dare say," says Mr.

Mrs. says, "Children love a game."

Hob says, "Hob's turn to give rewards."

"Hob will have a present specially from me," says Girl. "I'll make it or I'll buy."

Hob hopes she does not make mistakes and give him clothes to wear. If she did he would have to leave. He likes to live and work here.

"Dress him and he leaves his labor, Hob will find another neighbor," says Hob.

Budgie says, "Good-bye, perhaps."

Boy comes in with stray Black Dog. "I found him walking down the path," he says. "He has no collar, no tag, no home."

Black Dog licks his hand. Black Dog will not come near the fire.

"Hob wonders why," says Hob.

Budgie sings, "Perhaps it's Lob."

Hob looks again. "Lob is black," he says, "but Lob is Hob's friend. I think this is Black Dog."

Black Dog stays in a shadow. He looks. He stares. Mrs. says he ought to go outside.

But Black Dog sits and looks.

"Black Dog has gotten in," says Hob. "Hob will think."

Black Dog will not eat or drink. He will not go out.

"I wish I had not brought him in," says Boy. "But he walked so quietly along with me, so lost."

Black Dog lies in the shadows under the table.

"He should be in a kennel," says Mrs.

"Hob isn't sure of that," says Hob.

Black Dog licks Girl's hand. "What a dry lick," says Girl. "In the dark I almost see through him."

Black Dog is a pair of eyes. He looks at everyone. Budgie is so alarmed she puts her head in the water pot.

"There's dogs and Dogs," says Hob. "Black and Blacker."

The people go to bed. Black Dog stays under the table.

"Leave it to Hob," says Girl.

"Leave it to Hob," says Boy.

"Leave it to Hob," says Hob. Hob sets to work. It is not hard for him. He takes a strap and makes a

29

collar. He has another sixpence and he hangs that
on. Then he puts the collar on Black Dog. Black
Dog licks Hob, blinks his eyes, and says that now
he's dressed he'll go.

"It's the same for you as it is for Hob," says Hob.

Hob opens the door. Black Dog goes to do his
work, to help people cross the street, to make

sure they find their way, to keep travelers safe in rocky places.

"That's that," says Hob, shutting the door. "Come out, Budgie."

Budgie comes out. Budgie barks.

"Just like home," says Hob. He finds the reward Girl left him, a candy stick. He takes it to his cutch, or den, to eat it. In the house there are only shadows with no eyes.

HOB AND THE STRANGE BABY

Who rocks Baby's cradle when no one is in the room?

"It's Hob," says Baby, but even Hob does not understand his words.

"It's Hob," says Budgie, but even Budgie does not understand her words.

"It's Hob," say Boy and Girl, but no one believes it.

"Hob does," says Hob. "Hob likes Baby. I wonder why, because it isn't any use. No better than Budgie." Budgie scowls.

Hob rocks the cradle. Baby sings.

Hob gets his reward by the fireside each night and hopes he never is given clothes. He says, "Never give him leather or thread, or into the weather he will tread."

Baby does not always sing.

"I hope he's well," says Hob.

"Perhaps his teeth are growing," says Mrs.

"Baby doesn't need teeth," says Hob, and has a look. He opens Baby's mouth.

"His teeth are big," says Hob, taking his fingers away. He rocks the cradle. Baby snores.

"Baby is a little strange," says Girl. "Not himself."

"He's growing long," says Mrs. "He's not quite
so fat."

"He is still bald," says Boy.

"That's how he's born," says Mrs.

"He's eating quite a lot," says Mr. "Day and night,
night and day."

Hob has another look. Baby has a look at him. "Baby looks too hard at Hob," says Hob. "Maybe Hob looked too hard at him."

Now Baby does not sing at all. Baby complains. He shrieks when Budgie sings.

"That's sensible," says Hob. "But strange." He looks at Baby's feet. They are long and skinny, leathery and brown, and rather worn.

"Hob wonders," says Hob. "Hob does."

That night Hob is sure he sees smoke rising from the cradle. He creeps across and there is Baby smoking Hob's best pipe, puff, puff.

"This is a Changeling," says Hob. "I'll send it back and get the proper baby. Now, what can do the trick?"

He finds his nightly gift. It is an egg. "Hob loves an egg," he says, "and tonight most of all."

First he breaks the egg and eats the yolk and white. Then he draws the fire up and makes it warm. He says out loud, for Changeling to hear, "We'll have a pot of tea. Would you like that?"

Changeling pretends to be Baby. He does not

want to be found out. But Hob knows how to send
Changeling home.

Hob puts water in the eggshells and stands them
on the fire. He stands the big teapot in the hearth.

"In a minute," says Hob, "there'll be plenty for all."

"Nonsense," says the Changeling. "In all my long
life I never saw tea made in eggshells."

35

"Up you get," says Hob. "You have been found out." And the Changeling jumps from the cradle and goes up the chimney, taking Hob's best pipe with him. A moment later Baby knocks at the door. Hob brings him in and rocks his cradle. Baby sings.

"That's that," says Hob. "Hob knows a thing or two."

HOB AND MUMP

Boy and Girl know that Hob lives underneath the stairs. Mr. says, "Nonsense." Mrs. says, "What lovely fun." But Boy and Girl know that if they put a finger in a spyhole in the wood a little hand takes hold of it and gives a tiny squeeze.

"That's Hob," they say. "It's him."

"It's Hob," says Hob. "It's me."

All day he sleeps. At night he comes out and sees to things about the house and looks for his reward. Tonight he gets a buttered crust of bread. He bites it but it is hard to swallow. "They do their best for Hob," says Hob. He wonders why he cannot swallow simple crust.

The house is much too quiet. The clock ticks, the fire sleeps, the tap drips, the wind drives by. But it is much too quiet. Hob listens to it.

Baby is fast asleep. Budgie is not saying anything.

"That's not like Budgie," says Hob.

Budgie is standing on her perch. She is not eating, she is not playing, she does not ring her bell.

"Too quiet for Hob," says Hob.

"And Baby is too hot. I think there's something about."

And roundabout Hob looks. "Hob thinks Baby is too plump," he says.

Budgie cannot put her head underneath her wing. A Budgie tear drops from her eye.

Hob looks. Hob finds. Hob grabs.

Hob holds a roundish, softish thing that rolls about the room. It has no face, but all the same it scowls at him and slides out from his hand. Hob takes the fireguard and traps it against the wall.

"What are you?" he asks. "Hob wants to know. Tell Hob."

"I'm Mump," says roundish, softish thing. "I talked to Baby and to Budgie and gave them mumps. Now I have to go upstairs and leave my presents there. So let me go."

"Not yet," says Hob. He keeps Mump prisoner while he thinks. And after he has thought he remembers what to do. He goes outside, and by the waterside he searches until he finds a certain smooth, washed stone with a hole self-bored from front to back. Hob looks through and sees a distant star. "Hob's found it," he says, and hurries back.

He shows the stone to Mump. "You will have to
go," says Hob. "Before you go, take your present back
from Baby."

"Yes," says Mump. He has to, with a stone like
that. He does it. He has to go or be forever in that
stone. On the way he takes the present back from
Baby. Hob hangs the stone in the doorway. Mump

39

has to keep away. He cannot crawl through the stone. He has to stay out.

"Good," says Hob. "But my face aches."

"And so does mine," says Budgie. And Hob is sorry. He forgot poor Budgie. He goes up to her cage, and there he kindly chews birdseed soft for her.

Baby wakes up well, without a single mump.

HOB AND THE TEMPER

Hob lies in his cozy place underneath the stairs.

He hears Mr. say to a visitor, "This is Mrs., here are Boy and Girl and Baby. And in there is Hob, who is imaginary."

Hob puts out his head. "I'm not," he says. No one hears him. "I wish Hob was more real," he says.

"Told you so," laughs Budgie. "Hob isn't really there."

Hob scowls, feeling cross. He goes to sleep again. He wakes up feeling sad. Something is not right. He hears Boy and Girl quarreling at tea about the last teacake, and Baby cries, and someone gets a slap.

"Hob can tell," says Hob. "Bad times have come. Today they will give me the last present." They give him something every night. He thinks it will be things to wear, and if it is he will have to leave.

"It happens to Hob," he says. He stamps about the room. He slams the door of his cupboard.

He trips over something in the corner of the room.

"Mind how you go, Hob," growls Budgie.

"What has tripped Hob?" says Hob. "If that's the best they can do for me I'll be glad to go." *41*

"Temper, temper," says Budgie.

And Hob understands his bad feelings.

"I'm not cross," he says. "Hob is never angry. Hob is calm. But someone's temper has been lost and left lying on the floor."

"You leave me alone," says Temper, in a horrible way. "Or you'll be sorry, sorry, sorry."

Hob steps back. It is a bad temper he has found. He must be careful.

"Steady, Hob," he says. "Hob, think."

Hob thinks. He knows he must get rid of Temper. But the way to do it is quite hard for him.

"Budgie," he says, "Hob can't do it all alone."

"I can't do it at all," says Budgie. "Get rid of it. If it comes near me my feathers will fall out."

"We have to count backward," says Hob. "From five and twenty, like blackbirds in a pie. I can't count all alone. You start, feather duster, with the biggest number."

"Which is it?" says Budgie.

"Twenty-five," says Hob. "I think."

Budgie says, "Twenty-five." Hob works it out and says, "Twenty-four." He wakes Budgie, and she says, "Twenty-three."

Temper begins to move toward the door. Hob and
Budgie go on counting. They must not get it wrong.
"Eighteen, seventeen," they say.

Temper stands in the porch. "Eight, seven," say
Hob and Budgie.

Temper gets to the garden gate. "Three, two,
one," say Hob and Budgie. "Zero."

"Liftoff," says Temper, and goes stamping down the road.

"Thank you, Budgie," says Hob. He takes his reward, the buttery teacake Boy and Girl fought over. He gives Budgie currants from it.

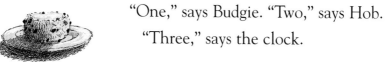

"One," says Budgie. "Two," says Hob.

"Three," says the clock.

HOB AND THE COUGH

"Poor Hob," the children say, "he can't be well."

"We heard him cough," say Girl and Boy.

"Nonsense," says Mr., "there's no such thing as Hob."

"Let them have their fun," says Mrs.

Hob is in his cupboard underneath the stairs. He hears them all. "Hob did not cough," he says. "There's something going about, that's all."

At night he comes out to look. Budgie sings.

"Quiet please, Hob's listening," says Hob.

"Listening to me," says Budgie, and sings a little trill.

"Hush," says Hob. "Listen. Did you hear that?"

There was a little trill from someone else, a little song.

"Something singing back," says Budgie, "because I sing so well." And then she sings a dreadful note, like rusty iron wire.

From the fireside there comes a croaking tune, half song, half splutter.

"That's Cough," says Hob. "Hob doesn't know he's there until he gets in someone's song."

"Gurr," sings Budgie, swinging upside down to cough.

"Well, hang in there," says Hob. "Hob will look by the fireside."

By the fireside a little cricket sits. He tries to sing, but every time he does, the Cough starts with him.

"Saw, saw, saw," goes Cricket.

"Hack, hack, hack," goes Cough.

"Think, think, think," goes Hob. Hob thinks.

"When they come down in the morning," says Cough, "I'll jump on.Mr., Mrs., Boy, Girl, and Baby. All of them."

Hob walks about thinking.

He grows tired of thinking.

Budgie goes, "Hisk, hisk, hisk."

Cricket goes, "Husk, husk, husk."

Hob gives up. He does not know what to do.

Hob goes to see what present has been left for him
tonight. He thinks, "If it is clothes I'll go. If I can't
get rid of a simple cough I'm not fit to stay."

In the bowl where gifts are put he finds a little
bottle and a tiny spoon. In the bottle there is
something black and sticky, sweet and strong. Hob
knows what it is. How kind the people are to him.

47

It is cough syrup, cough cure. Hob takes the bottle first to Cricket.

"Open wide," he says, and Cricket swallows down. Out jumps Cough.

"Open wide," says Hob to Budgie. Budgie opens wide and swallows down. Cough jumps out.

"Open wide," says Hob. Cough opens wide the door and goes out, and right away. "That's cured that," says Hob, and drinks a drop himself, in case.

Hob and the Storm

Mr. takes a family photograph. The camera makes a
bright light at them.

Mrs. smiles and hopes her hair is tidy.

Boy frowns a bit and hopes he is printed grown up.

Girl has her tongue out, trying to lick her chin.

Baby looks cross-eyed but happy.

Mr. looks at the picture when it comes back.

"It's spoiled," he says. "The light got in."

Hob, in his cupboard underneath the stairs, thinks something different.

"It's Hob," says Boy. "Of course."

"He's part of the family," says Girl.

"Nonsense," says Mr. "The camera cannot lie. It must be broken."

The children know it is Hob, their friend. They put the picture up for him to see.

Hob looks. "Dear me," he says, "I've nothing on. Hob only dresses when he goes away."

"All nonsense," says Mr.

Mrs. puts her thumb over that part of the picture.

Hob gets up at night and goes about the house.

"Smile please," he says to Budgie. Budgie hides her face, all shy. She has been frightened by her own shadow when the camera winked.

Hob can't be seen in day or dark, but only in between, dawn and dusk or moonlight.

Budgie can see him now. And then a bright light comes and she can't. She sees her shadow on the wall. She thinks it is a hawk. She falls into her seed box. The shadow goes in with her.

"What was that?" says Hob. "Another photograph?"
And the bright light comes again.

The light comes sparkling at the window. It comes
in and sits on the knives and spoons, and twinkles all
round the room.

"Perhaps they are making a film and I'm the star,"
says Budgie.

"That would be a horror film," says Hob. "No. Lightning has come in, that's all."

Lightning flashes round the fire. Lightning crackles round the clock. Lightning makes the kettle boil. Lightning laughs. "I've gotten away," he says. And he makes Budgie's cage all prickly.

"This is wild, naughty lightning," says Hob. "And it

is inside the house. I'm off," and he goes to the door.

Lightning sits on the doorknob. Hob touches it. His hair stands on end. His teeth feel loose.

He opens the door, but he does not dare go out. Something big is there. Something is walking very large and heavy. Something monstrous in the garden is treading in the trees.

Lightning has had enough of playing on its own.

"Mother," it shouts, "Mother Thunder," and goes like lightning to the big thing outside, Mother Thunder.

"Thank you," says Mother Thunder, very rumbly. And Hob goes in. He climbs up with Budgie and they both tidy their feathers and their hair in her mirror, in the dark. Outside Mother Thunder rolls away and little Lightning sparkles in her arms.

HOB AND EGGY PALMER

Boy and Girl know that Hob is there. The family feels complete when he comes out to sit with them.

Tonight he shyly squats on the hardest cushion, farthest from the fire. All the cushions are hard tonight.

"He's here," says Girl. She does not look in case she frightens him.

"He's there," says Boy. He does not point. It would not be polite.

"Nonsense," says Mr. "And it's time to go to bed."

Boy and Girl go to bed. "Goodnight, Hob," they say.

Hob has just gotten up, from his cutch, or cupboard, underneath the stairs. Hob thinks there is a problem in the house.

"Did you lay an egg, Budgie?" he asks, when they are alone.

Budgie blushes. "Not me," she whispers.

"Good," says Hob. He knows there is an eggy problem.

"What a thing to ask!" says Budgie.

When the family is all in bed Hob finds what is wrong.

Someone has been boiling eggs. Baby had an egg for tea.

In the water the egg had cracked.

Eggy Palmer had come out.

First a long white finger.

Then a broad white hand.

Then Eggy Palmer his full self came swimming from the shell, hard and ready, ready and set.

"Set and go, Hob thinks," says Hob.

Eggy Palmer waits in the kitchen to make the custard lumpy. He will dip his broad smooth hand in it and spoil it.

He will put bones in the potatoes.

He will put long blobs like cloth in the milk.

He will stain spoons black and put hard lumps between forks.

He will make spaghetti stick together.

He will make jelly lumpy.

He has already been in the cushions.

Now he is in the sink, using his brain, having a think beside the drain.

Hob thinks too. Eggy Palmer will have to go. But Hob does not tell him so, because that might make him cross.

Hob is kind to him. Beware of Hob when Hob is
being nice. It is best when Hob speaks sharply to
you, very near unkind.

"I'll help you out of there," says Hob. "You might
get washed away."

"Thank you," says Eggy Palmer. "Then I can get
to work."

56

"Just climb in this eggshell, where you came from," says Hob. "I'll lift you from the sink."

Eggy Palmer climbs in. Hob puts his thumb on top to keep him in. "Hob knows," says Hob, and goes to the waterside and sends Eggy down the stream, away and away.

"How far to custard?" shouts Eggy.

Of course it is very far. But Eggy comes out happy, and he is quite good for frogspawn.

Hob goes home. He eats his gift, a roasted apple. There is something knotted in the middle. It is the core. Budgie eats the pips.

HOB AND SOOTKIN

Who sat by the fire one icy winter's morning, puffing an old clay pipe?

"Who is it?" says Mr. "I smell a sort of goblin tobacco."

"It's Hob," says Girl. "I know the smell."

"It's Hob," says Boy. "It's cold today."

"It's Hob," says Hob. "Hob has been found out, so he'll go back to his cutch underneath the stairs."

Hob goes to his cupboard so quick, before he's seen, that he leaves the old clay pipe behind.

"You've frightened him away," says Girl.

"There was nothing there," says Mr.

But Boy puts the old clay pipe in a safe place. He knows and Girl knows. Hob knows.

That night there is worse than goblin tobacco making smoke.

The chimney is not working well. Puffs of smoke go up, but puffs of smoke come down. Puffs of smoke are in the room.

"All that soot," says Mrs. "And Baby turning black."

Smoke gets in their eyes.

Budgie coughs. "I'm trying to give it up," she says.

The family goes to bed. Budgie puts her head under her wing. The air is fresher there.

Hob comes out. He thinks it is his fault. He goes to find his old clay pipe.

He finds it. He expects the smoke has come from that. But it is not so.

He goes to the fireplace. Smoke comes down. Hob gets it in his mouth. It gets in his ears.

It seems to speak to him.

"Hob hears you," says Hob. "Your name is Sootkin. You live in the chimney."

Sootkin rustles in the chimney. Black specks fall down.

"You will have to go," says Hob.

Sootkin shakes a chimney pot. "Never," says Sootkin.

"Hob says yes," says Hob.

Sootkin scampers up and down the flue. Lumps of black fall down and smell foul.

"Hob thinks what to do," says Hob.

He remembers then. He knows. The cure is something he does not like, but he bravely touches it. He brings salt from the salt pot and sprinkles it on Sootkin's toes.

Sootkin does not like it either. He whizzes round and round.

Hob sprinkles salt on Sootkin's head.

Sootkin roars. Sootkin rushes out of the top of the chimney. He goes so fast the chimney pot splits apart and falls.

"Hob is pleased," says Hob.

Budgie brings her head out and spits black spit.

Hob sweeps up. When that is done he finds his gift, a mug of ale. "That slakes the soot," he says.

In the morning Mr. finds the broken chimney pot and thinks that that was what was wrong. Hob knows better.

HOB AND HINKY PUNK

Hob likes the twilight at dusk and dawn. He sees best then, and can be seen. Bright day and black dark are not good for him.

"We see him in the shadows," says Boy.

"Or moonlight," says his sister, Girl.

"Just when I've got my eyes closed," shouts Budgie.

"You're all talking nonsense," says Mr.

Hob listens from his cupboard. "They are talking about Hob," says Hob.

At night he creeps from his cutch, his cupboard.

He waits. Budgie snores. A mouse comes out and asks for quiet.

In a corner of the room something seems to grow out of the stone floor.

Little things like leaves of grass come up, blue and bright, red and shining, long and longer.

It is not grass, but hair. And the head comes out, and the rest of a little creature, all bright and shining.

Hob shades his eyes. "And who are you?" he asks.

"I'm Hinky Punk," the creature says.

Budgie wakes. "Go away," she says.

"Go to roost, sparrow," says Hinky Punk. He says

to Hob, "What's up, Grandad? You don't have to stay.
Hinky Punk rules okay."

"This is Hob's home," says Hob.

And the mice say, "This is our mousehold. Bless
this mouse."

"Hinky Punk has come to town," says Hinky Punk.

"I was getting nowhere in the swamp. Here I am until I leave."

"What shall we do?" ask the mice.

Budgie bites her nails.

Hob shuts his eyes and thinks.

Hinky Punk goes running round the room, jumping on the table, clattering in the hearth, being so bright.

64

"Vandal," says Budgie.

Hob thinks.

"Candle," says Budgie.

Baby wakes and cries.

"Scandal," says Budgie.

"Featherbrain," says Hob. He is thinking. Then he has thought.

He talks to the mice. He explains what they can do. "It's the same for Hinky Punk as it is for Hob," he says. "Just as it was for Black Dog."

The mice begin their work. "It is a secret," they tell Hinky Punk, when he comes round to watch. "Stand there so we can see to thread the needle."

They thread and they sew, and they cut and they stitch, and their mousework is a suit of clothes for Hinky Punk. He has to put them on.

"Good gear," he says.

And when he has them on he has to go. "Cheers," he says, and stamps off in new boots.

"Good riddance," say the mice, and Budgie, and Hob.

HOB AND SLEEPYHEAD

Hob looks with a bright eye through the spyhole in his cutch, or cupboard.

"Something is looking out," says Mrs. "It will be a spider. Ugh."

"Hob looked out," says Boy.

"He lives there in his cutch," says Girl.

"Hob looked out," says Hob. "But he doesn't see so well."

"I can't see anything," says Mr.

"You're worse than me," says Hob. "And I have a headache, too."

Girl says, "I am so sleepy."

Baby nods his head.

Mr. closes his eyes.

Boy gazes into the fire.

Budgie says she is losing her mind.

"I know," says Hob.

Mrs. knits three stitches backward in the wrong color on the poker instead of the needle. "How tired I am," she says. "We'll all go to bed."

Hob gets up. His poor head aches. Budgie sits with her eyes tight closed, too weary to put her head under her wing.

Hob thinks he is dreaming. Then he thinks that something is dreaming him.

Hob thinks his headache is too bad. He goes upstairs and wakes Mrs. She gives him headache tea, and he feels better then.

He looks in the mirror. He sees his face. It looks and feels fuzzy. He sees on his head a round black thing like a little hat. He knows it is not clothes. But what is it?

He takes it off and sees it is Sleepy-head. Sleepyhead has put a hand on everyone and made them sleep—Mr., Mrs., Baby, Boy, Girl, Budgie, and the mouse.

Hob stayed awake and his head hurt.

"What are you doing here?" he asks. "Hob wants to know. His eyes want mending or he would have seen you sooner."

"I have to sleep somewhere," says Sleepyhead. "But hedgehogs prickled me and woke me up. I'll sleep here, Hob."

"This is Hob's house," says Hob.

"Don't send me back to hedgehogs," says Sleepyhead. "They have spiny dreams."

"Hob will help," says Hob, and goes looking for help.

There is Dormouse in the shed. "I can't sleep,"
he says. "Will Mrs. give me sleeping tea?"

"Hob gives you this," says Hob, and puts
Sleepyhead beside him. They curl up together, snore,
and snore alike.

68   Hob's headache goes. Inside, beside the fire, he

finds his present, a pair of glasses. Now he can see sharp again. He looks at Budgie.

"It's a monster," Budgie shouts, and rings her bell.

In the morning Mrs. asks which child had headache tea at night.

"It was Hob," say Boy and Girl. "He says thank you very much."

"I do," says Hob, sleepy in his cutch.

HOB AND TOOTH FAIRY

Who had bad dreams in a cupboard under the stairs?

"It's Hob," say Boy and Girl. "That's his cutch, where he lives."

"It's the drains," says Mr. "Drains are real, at least."

Hob was dreaming. He dreams all day, in his sleep. Sometimes he wakes up.

"Nothing like a good dream," he says.

Baby dreams at night. Baby wakes.

"That was bad dream," says Baby. Baby tells the house.

"Poor thing," says Mrs. "His teeth are coming through. Look."

Hob says, "Perhaps Hob's teeth are coming through. Here's a gap, and there's a gap." But perhaps Hob's teeth are like that.

Girl puts a fingertip in her mouth and smiles round it. "I have a loose tooth," she says. "Feel it wobbling."

"We have a problem," says Hob. Girl lets him feel her tooth. She trusts him. He trusts her. The tooth is loose backward and forward.

"Hob has work to do," says Hob.

Next he looks in Baby's mouth. There is a little lump, but the tooth has not come up. Hob rubs the place and Baby dribbles with delight.

He looks inside Girl's smile. The tooth is loose up and down. Hob knows what to do and looks for the thing to do it with. Girl's tooth hangs by a thread.

Baby is extremely cross.

"A toothling, not a changeling," says Hob. He has to go on looking for what he needs.

Baby gets a rash. Girl says she cannot eat anything she does not like, with a tooth like that.

Hob finds a silver thing he wants. Now he is ready. He waits.

Suddenly Girl says, "It has gone. It has fallen out." There on the table lies her tooth.

"Ah," says Hob, still waiting.

"Eat your potato, Girl," says Mrs.

Baby's rash vanishes. In his mouth is a little white bud, a tooth coming up.

Everybody looks. Boy and Girl think the little bud may open like a flower.

Hob is busy. He knows what came out with Girl's tooth and flew up to settle near Budgie, waiting for a new home. Hob sees Tooth Fairy.

"Is it here?" asks Tooth Fairy, looking longingly at Budgie.

"No," says Hob. "It lost its teeth long ago."
Budgie hears that and snarls. Hob takes the Fairy
down to Baby, and Baby smiles.

"Pay for my old tooth," says Fairy, "and I'll go
to work again, growing a new set for Baby."

Hob takes the silver thing, a coin, and puts it
where Girl has left her tooth, in a glass of water.

His gift tonight is a long white pipe, a yard of clay. It fits the gap in his teeth, better than a tooth.

Upstairs Mr.'s teeth are in a glass of water. He will never get a silver penny for any of them.

HOB AND CLOCKSTOP

"How strange," says Mrs., the last day of February, at time for tea.

"How strange," say Boy and Girl. "Hob has laid the breakfast table."

"Breakfast," says Mr. "What nonsense. If there was such a person as Hob he would have to go."

"Hob's mad," says Budgie.

"Hob is doing his best," says Hob. "They're late. It's breakfast o'clock by the Grandfather."

"Tock," says Grandfather. "Tick."

"The clock is wrong," says Mr. He tries to set it right.

The weights run down. The pendulum goes clatter. Something mechanical is the matter.

"Never mind," says Budgie. "I will ring my bell," and she rings half and quarter past twenty-seven o'clock.

At night Hob comes out.

"What's the trouble, Grandfather?" he asks. "Hob wants to know. Are you on strike?"

Grandfather groans. "I've chilblains on my hands," he says, "and a pain in my bell. I think I'm two days slow."

"You've run down," says Hob. He looks inside.

"Tick," says Grandfather. Hob puts a finger in.

"Tock," says Grandfather. "I think you've hit the place."

"Something has crawled in," says Hob. "It is tangled round your hickory dickory dock. It is a Clockstop."

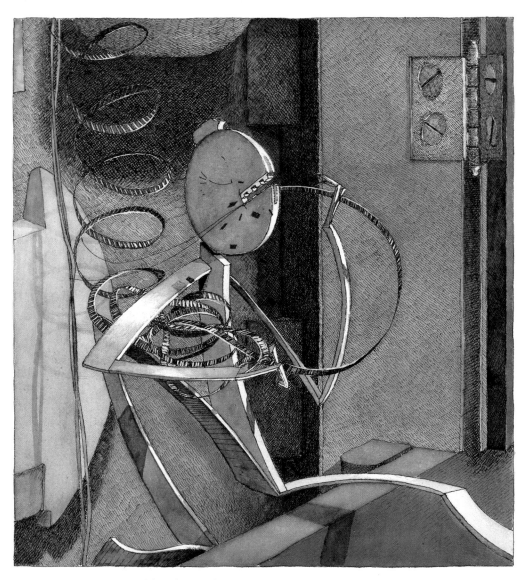

"Oh, ding, dong," says Grandfather.

"Come out, Clockstop," says Hob. He pulls.

"I'm stopping here," says Clockstop, "eating seconds and minutes."

"I can spare a few," says Grandfather.

"I'll eat the hours and the days," says Clockstop.

76   "Take them and let me go," says Grandfather.

"I'll eat the phases of the moon," says Clockstop.

The pendulum falls off. "I'll eat the date," says Clockstop. "Whole years at once."

Then Hob remembers what date it is, what day.

"Don't be greedy, Clockstop," he says. "We all have to share. There's lots of us and we want a few minutes each."

"All right," says Clockstop. "I might get time-ache."

"Have today every time it comes," says Hob.

"Yum yum yes," says Clockstop. "Every year I'll come back." And out he comes, a long and springy, ringy thing. He goes away quite pleased with a handful of milliseconds to eat on the way.

"Tick tock, tick tock," says Grandfather clock. "I'm mended and I'm well, ding, dong, bell."

Hob gets a candle for a gift. "I could see to mend midnight now," he says.

Clockstop comes again next February 29th, in a leap year four years later. Hob worked it well. Clockstop is a long time gone.

HOB AND WUMP

In the night Hob comes from his cutch, his cupboard underneath the stairs.

"He does his good deeds then," says Boy.

"And gets a reward," says Girl.

Mr. says, "Nonsense."

But Hob comes out. Tonight he rocks the cradle. Baby has been cross all day and does not want to sleep.

Budgie rocks her cage and rattles.

Baby was going off to sleep. He wakes up again and whimpers.

"Hush, Budgie," says Hob. "Hush, Baby."

Budgie stamps about her perch.

"Shush," says Hob. "Hob is busy."

"It's not me," says Budgie.

Hob rocks the cradle. Baby forgets how cross he is. His eyes close.

Rock, rock, gently rock, goes the cradle. Hob feels sleepy too.

The cradle rocks faster.

Tap, tap, quickly tap, it goes.

"Not so hasty," says Hob.

Baby blows a bubble. Pop goes the bubble. Out comes a shout.

Bang, bang, trample bang, goes the cradle.

"Yow, yow, yow," says Baby.

Hob is out of breath. "Puff, puff, puff," he says. "There's more than baby in the cradle."

Thump, thump, rockety thump, goes the cradle. Baby falls out. Hob catches him.

"I'll hold him," says Budgie.

"The bird is mad," says Hob. "But we have a problem here for Hob to solve."

Wump goes the cradle.

Cradle stops, but Wump goes on. Wump in the kitchen, Wump in the hall; Wump in the passage, Wump up the wall; Wump in the chairs, Wump on the stairs. Says Hob, "It won't do at all."

He puts Baby back to sleep. "Sing to him, hen," he says to Budgie.

"Go to sleep, little egg," sings Budgie.

"The bird's an idiot," says Hob.

Wump is wumping in the cellar.

"Why?" asks Hob. "This is my house."

"Looking for Grandwump," says Wump. "Mr. Earthquake. And there's Auntie Sonic Boom, and Cousin Noisy Neighbor, and my little sister, Footsteps In The Night."

"They don't live here," says Hob. "Try down
the road."

Wump climbs the cellar steps. The whole house
shakes. Budgie's knees molt. Hob's teeth rattle. He
opens the front door.

Wump goes out. Wump, wump, bumpety bump,
down the garden path. His family calls to him.

Hob finds his present from Boy and Girl, an electric torch. While Baby sleeps and Budgie squawks, Hob puts back the seeds Wump shook out of the garden.

"Hob's work is never done," he says.

HOB AND HOTFOOT

"Hob will be cross," says Girl.

"But that is nonsense," says Mr. He is using a blue bowl to put dead matches in.

"We put our present for Hob in that," says Boy. "Hob is our household friend."

"Imaginary beings do not mind," says Mr.

Hob in his cutch, his den underneath the stairs, minds very much. Presents are presents, given not bought. But if it's clothes, Hob goes.

That night he does not know what is his.

"All gone," says Budgie.

"You get your wages in birdseed," says Hob. "They're fattening you up. They don't keep you because they like you. They like me."

But the blue bowl is full of spent matches and nasty black stuff from Mr.'s pipe.

Hob picks up the bowl and puts it down. Hob is sad. Hob will do no work. Hob goes back to bed.

"Come out, come out," sings Budgie. "There's something about."

Hob will not come out. But the next day he

is sorry when he hears the family talking.

"What dreadful marks," says Mrs. "How did they come?"

Hob wonders what she means. "Has Hob done it?" he wonders.

Something has been on tabletop and sideboard, cupboard top and floorboard.

White circles are lying everywhere. Hob finds them when he comes out. White rings appear on polished places.

"Hotfoot has been here," says Hob. "You did not tell me, Budgie."

"He has not been up here," says Budgie. But she is wrong. Hotfoot trod in her water and it boiled away.

Hotfoot walks across the washing hung to dry and burns brown rings in it.

Hob knows what to do. He goes for his blue bowl. Tonight there is a splendid gift in it, making up for yesterday. It is a sweet plum pie with a sugary crust.

Hob puts it on the table. It is still hot. It leaves a hard white ring. "Oh dear," says Hob, and eats the pie.

When it has gone he takes the bowl outside. It is the time for cold moonlight. He fills the bowl with that and brings it in.

"Warm up my custard," he says to Hotfoot.

Hotfoot comes to scorch the custard. He gets into the bowl, into the moonlight lying cold in the bowl.

Hotfoot freezes. Hotfoot turns solid with cold. Hob picks him out, and at the garden gate he rolls him down the road.

"That's a different sort of bowl," says Hob.

When Hotfoot has finished rolling he falls flat. In

the morning workmen think he is a hole and put a lid on him.

In the house Hob washes all the marks away with moonlight. They go from desk and doorway, bench and stairway. All except the one Hob made himself, which will not scrub away.

"Hob's autograph," Hob says. "If I could write."

HOB AND DUSTY

Mrs. takes the carpet off the stairs and rolls it out on the garden path.

"I can't get the dust out of it," she says. Dust flies over the garden.

"Stop it," says Mr. "My cabbages."

"Hob might be in it," says Girl.

"Nonsense," says Mr.

Mrs. goes thump, thump with a carpet paddle.

But Hob is in his cutch under the top step.

Boy and Girl go to look. They mean no harm.

The top step is loose. They do not mean to be impolite.

Hob hears the boards begin to rattle.

Boy and Girl do not mean to be unkind. They love Hob around the house.

Hob hears a nail begin to creak, creak, creak.

"Go back in your cage, Budgie," he calls. Budgie is offended. Hob thinks her voice is like a nail pulling out. She mutters like a clockwork bird.

Hob sees daylight coming in. He leaves the cutch through his own front door. He hides inside the Grandfather clock.

"Do not tickle, tickle," says the clock.

"This happens every hundred years or so," says Hob.

"I remember," says the clock. "It was a Tuesday."
Budgie thinks it was last week. There was Tuesday then.

Boy and Girl have lifted up the step. Hob's little
bed is hard and humpy, short and lumpy.

Beside it is a dusty floor. Dusty gets up and looks at
Boy and Girl.

"We'll sweep it out," says Girl.

When they go for brush and pan Dusty climbs out
and down the stairs. He is made of fluff, feather,
threads, and bits. He goes into a corner.

He leaves crumb, grime, dirt, and grit wherever
he goes.

Boy sweeps the cutch floor. Girl dusts Hob's
things, his pipes and torch, his gifts.

They feel his wooden bed, his bony pillow.

They put the top step back. They clear the stairs of fluff and feather, they clear the floor of crumb and grime. Mrs. puts the stair carpet back.

Hob stays inside the clock all day. At night he comes out. He has some sweeping of his own to do. He has to be rid of Dusty.

Hob curls up in the dustpan. "Comfortable here," he says.

Dusty is molting hairy sand and grassy mud. Dusty climbs in beside Hob.

Hob carefully climbs out. Dusty shakes himself comfortable. Hob sneezes. Budgie sneezes. The clock sneezes midnight. Every sneeze means go. The door sneezes open.

Dusty sneezes. He falls to pieces. When he does Hob picks up the dustpan and takes it outside before Dusty comes together again.

Dusty comes together too late, in the dustbin.

"This is home," says Dusty.

"Good night," says Hob. He goes in. Boy and Girl have left him a cushion for a pillow. He goes to bed.

HOB AND HICKUP

Boy and Girl have Puppy in the house. He runs about and barks at Hob's cutch, or cupboard, under the stairs.

"Come away," says Girl. "Hob can't be nipped by you."

"I'd bite back," says Hob.

"Chase Baby," says Boy. "Baby thinks it's fun." Baby thinks it's fun.

"It's time for tea," says Mr. "Dogs outside. Give him a biscuit as he goes."

Girl gives him a pink one, Boy gives him a yellow one. Baby tries a pretty black one and drops it in a corner.

Then it is time for tea. Says Mrs., "Don't gobble it so quick."

Says Mr., "Hick." He's not the only one. Girl has Hickup too. Boy has such a big one they all laugh. Baby bounces up and down with it.

Boy gets a sugar lump with vinegar on it. He jumps on Girl and frightens Hickup from her.

Baby gets Hickup water made by Mrs. with a cinder from the fire.

Mr. has something from a bottle.

"That's best," he says.

"I could try that," says Hob.

"I don't believe in household spirits," says Mr., putting back the cork.

Boy and Girl and Baby, Mr. and Mrs. and Budgie go to bed.

Hob comes out.

There is Hickup in the curtains. "Beg your pardon," says Spider, covering her face with all her legs.

"Hickory, dickory, dock," goes the clock.

Budgie says, "Skwee, skwee, skwee, skwee." She thinks she is singing. "Skwee, hick," she goes, and knows she's not.

"Hold your breath a couple of days," says Hob.

Budgie drinks from the back of her water pot and wricks her neck.

"Hick," go the taties in the cellar.

"Hack," goes the poker by the fire.

"Hock," goes the jam inside the jar.

"Huck and ill-luck," says Hob. "Who's there? Tell Doctor Hob."

Hickup comes up, and Hickup comes down. Hickup comes across the floor, hop, hick, and jump.

"Stand still," says Hob.

"I can't," says Hickup. "I ate a pretty black biscuit behind the cradle, and we've all got it now."

"Stand still," says Hob. "Good boy, STAND STILL!"

91

Hickup stands still. His little tum goes hick and hock but he stands still.

"You've eaten dog biscuit," says Hob. "What's best for dogs?"

"Mmimm," goes Hickup, very quiet Hickup.

"Walkies," says Hob. "That's it." And Walkies is what it is, by Hob's left heel and down the garden path.

"Now run away," says Hob, and Hickup does, hickover the road, hickover the hedge. People think Indigestion's going by.

Inside, blue Budgie blushes pink. She turns burple. "It wasn't Hick at all," she says. "I've laid an egg."

"Hob loves an egg," says Hob. "Hob does."

"If we weren't friends," says Budgie, "I'd sometimes hate you."

Hob eats his gift, a sardine on the bone.